Bunny My Honey

For Susan

ISBN 0-439-07263-8

12 11 10 9 8 7 6 5 4 3 2 1   0 1 2 3 4 5/0

Printed in the U.S.A.   08

First Scholastic printing, January 2000

This book was typeset in Kabel Book Alt.
The pictures were done in watercolor and ink.

Bunny My Honey

Anita Jeram

SCHOLASTIC INC.

New York Toronto London Auckland Sydney
Mexico City New Delhi Hong Kong

Mommy Rabbit had a baby.

His name was Bunny.

He looked just like his mommy,

only smaller.

He had long ears,

a twitchy nose, and great big feet.

"Bunny, my Honey,"

Mommy Rabbit liked to call him.

Mommy Rabbit showed Bunny how to do special rabbity things,

like running and hopping,

digging and twitching his nose,

and thumping his great big feet.

Sometimes Bunny played with his best friends,
Little Duckling and Miss Mouse.
They played quack-quacky games,
squeaky games and thump-thump-thumpy games.

They sang, We're the little Honeys.
A little Honey is sweet.
Quack quack, squeak squeak,
Thump your great big feet!

If a game ever ended in tears,

as games sometimes do,

Mommy Rabbit made it better.

"Don't cry, my little Honeys,"
Mommy Rabbit said, "I'm right here."

But one day Bunny got lost.

Oh, how could such a bad thing happen?

Perhaps it was a game that went wrong.

Perhaps Bunny ran too far on his own.

But there he was,
just one lost Bunny.

The more Bunny looked for

his friends and his mommy

the more lost

and the more lost

and the more lost he became.

Bunny started to cry.

"Mommy, Mommy,

I want my mommy!

Mommy, Mommy,

I want my mommy!"

"Bunny, my Honey!"

What was that?

"Bunny, my Honey!

Bunny, my Honey!"

"Bunny, my Honey!"

"MOMMY!"

Mommy Rabbit picked Bunny

up and cuddled him.

She stroked his long ears.

She put her twitchy nose

on his twitchy nose.

She kissed his great big feet.

Bunny's ears and nose

and feet felt warm all over.

"I love you, Mommy,"
Bunny whispered.
"I love you, Bunny, my Honey,"
Bunny's mommy
whispered back,
"and I love my other
little Honeys, too."

On the way home, Bunny and Miss Mouse and Little Duckling sang their song.

We're the little Honeys.
A little Honey is sweet.
Quack quack, squeak squeak,
Thump your great big feet!

And Bunny was a
happy rabbit.